Shelty the Seashell's First Adventure

This book belongs to:

_____

Written by Kyle and Helena DeLuca

Illustrated by Helena DeLuca

Shelty the Seashell's First Adventure

Copyright© 2015 by Helena A. DeLuca

Illustrated by Helena A. DeLuca

Printed by CreateSpace, an Amazon.com Company
Available from Amazon.com, CreateSpace.com, and other retail outlets.
Published by Dorothy-Frances Books®

Library of Congress Control Number:
ISBN-13: 978-0692277348
ISBN-10: 069227734X

CONTENTS

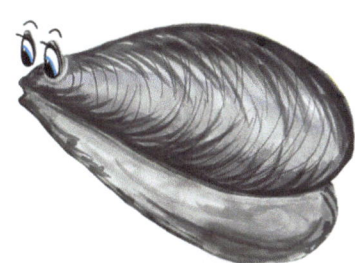

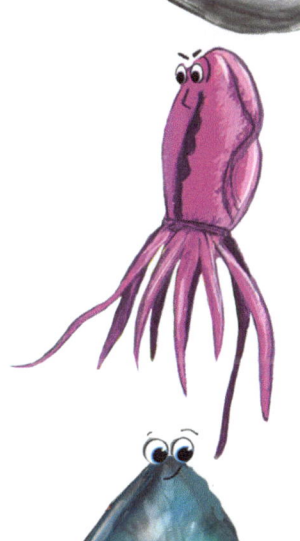

This book is dedicated to anyone to whom this story may bring a smile. It is also dedicated to my wonderful family, with special attention to my son Kyle, whose very creative middle-school Language Arts composition provided the basis and inspiration for this adaptation. Many of his original concepts and ideas have been maintained and blended into this illustrated version. *Helena A. DeLuca*

Introduction

What could it be?
Why is Shelty in the Shellhamas?
What exciting adventure
did he want to tell me about?
Dottie wondered.

Curious, Dottie hurried and finished up her chores with a sweep and a swoosh and a wipe and a whoosh. Then she threw on her new summer dress and got ready to fly to the Shellhamas to visit Shelty.

Dottie the dragonfly and Shelty had met one day when she had landed on a rock at the seashore to rest her shimmering wings. Shelty, a red abalone seashell, had floated peacefully ashore. The two found they had a lot in common even though they lived in two very different worlds, and they have been good friends ever since.

Shelty wrote to Dottie about a reward he had received for going on an exciting adventure. In the letter, he invited her to come visit him while he vacationed in the Shellhamas.

It was a breezy summer day—perfect for flying. Dottie enjoyed the help from the warm, gentle breeze as she flew to the Shellhamas. She spotted Shelty on the shore and glided over to join him.

The two friends chatted and caught up with one another as they rested comfortably on their beach lounges.

"I can't wait to hear about your exciting adventure, Shelty," Dottie said. "Let the story begin!"

Hello everybody!
My name is Shelty.

My actual name—my birth name, that is—is Shelton Q. Abalone. We abalone shells have a special feature: a shell with a curved row of open coils. My great-grandfather and I are the only two abalone shells in all of abalone history who were born with an *extra* **BLUE** nose coil. For this reason, my parents proudly named me after him.

I can't wait to tell you and my friend Dottie all about my fantastic first adventure...

It all started when I delivered a note to the Conch Colony Leader. I ended up going on an unexpected mission when I volunteered to rescue my friend Mick Mussel. The mission took me far beyond the part of the sea I call home. I'm actually not the adventurous type, being a rather common shell and all. Wait, let me start from the beginning.

I work at the *Sea-Urchin Post Office* and deliver packages and mail to the different shell colonies. One day last week, I drifted over to the Conch Colony with what looked like an ordinary letter. Just as I tossed it into the Conch Colony mail bin, I noticed it was marked "URGENT!"

I quickly took the letter back out of the mail bin and delivered it *personally* to the Conch Colony Leader.

When the Conch Colony Leader received the note, she called
for a special *Shell-Town Meeting*. She waited for all the shells
to gather and then read the note out loud.

Dear Conch Colony Leader,

Please find me a brave shell who can rescue my son. All those who were sent by King Neptune considered it too risky, so we haven't found someone brave enough. PLEASE HELP!

We will give a handsome reward to whomever you send.

Sincerely,

Mussel Colony Leader #153

P. S. He's at MUM's Cave

The worried Mussel Colony Leader arrived for the meeting too. He hoped a brave shell would volunteer to rescue his son, Mick Mussel. I thought, *What could the Mussel Colony Leader be thinking? MUM's Cave is the home of the feared sea monster!*

The water became very still. Not one shell uttered a peep until I screamed out, "I'LL VOLUNTEER!" before I could stop myself. The Conch Colony and Mussel Colony Leaders looked over to where I was floating. A chilling cold shiver ran down my coils even though the water was a warm seventy-eight degrees. All the other shells faded into the background as they attempted to disappear out of sight.

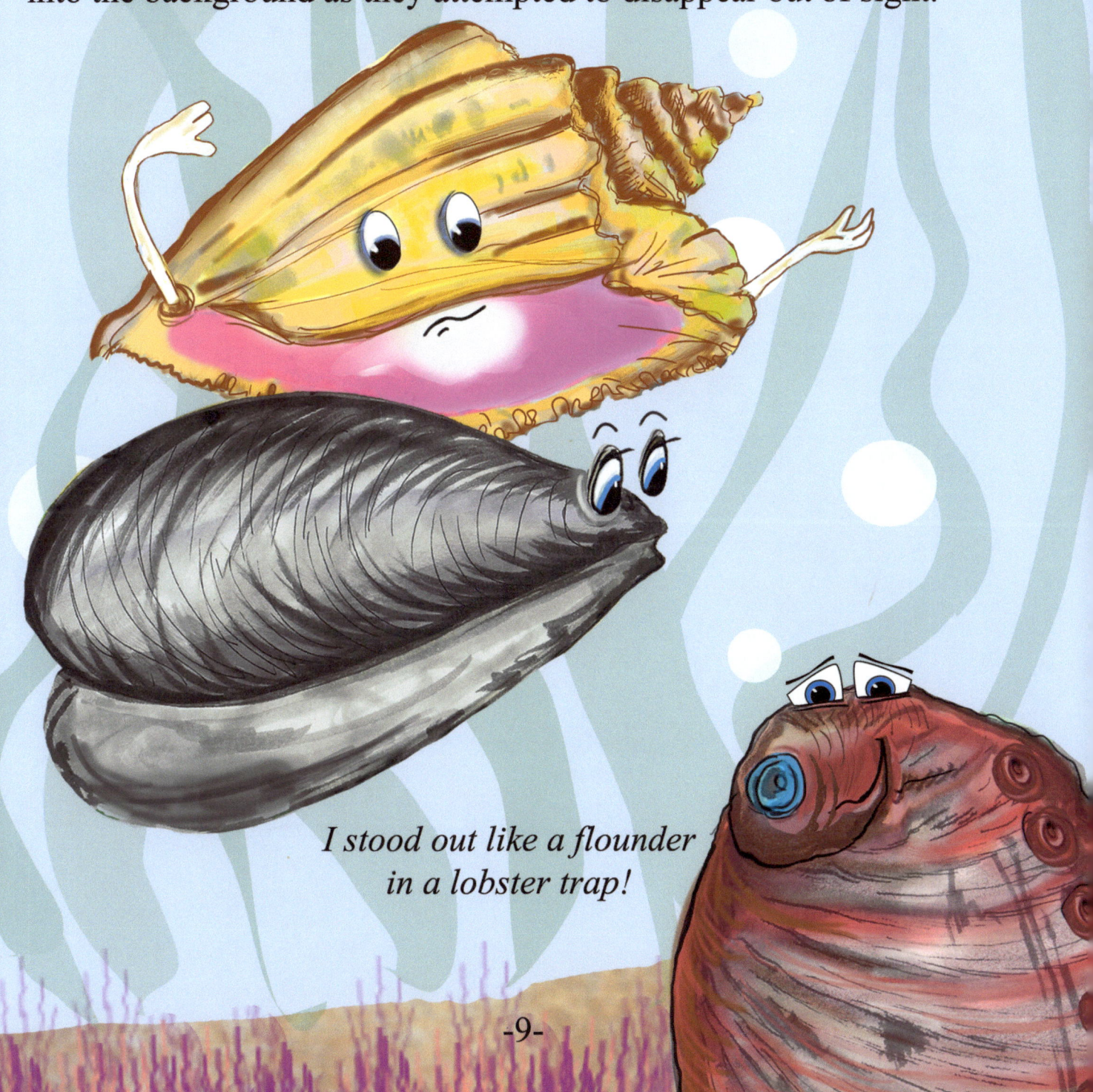

I stood out like a flounder in a lobster trap!

Shells shiver at the mere mention of the sea monster. No shells in their right minds want to go within a mega-shell length of MUM's Cave, yet—the reality suddenly hit me—I had j-just v-volunteered to do exactly that!

Eeek!!

I was scared coil-less. I almost couldn't breathe. Water droplets dripped down my shell. My shell began beating fast. As the Conch Colony Leader finished reading the note, I imagined that I heard my great-grandfather talking to me. He had a calming, reassuring voice that echoed like a sound wave through the water.

"Never let fear stand in the way of doing the right thing."

-11-

I had spent many summers with Mick Mussel at *Shrimp Sea Camp*. The thought of him shelled-in at MUM's Cave with the sea monster was too scary. I admit I felt a bit *clammy*, but, well, I also felt brave. After all, rescuing Mick *was* the right thing to do. Besides, I figured that with the reward, I would have some extra money to go on a nice vacation.

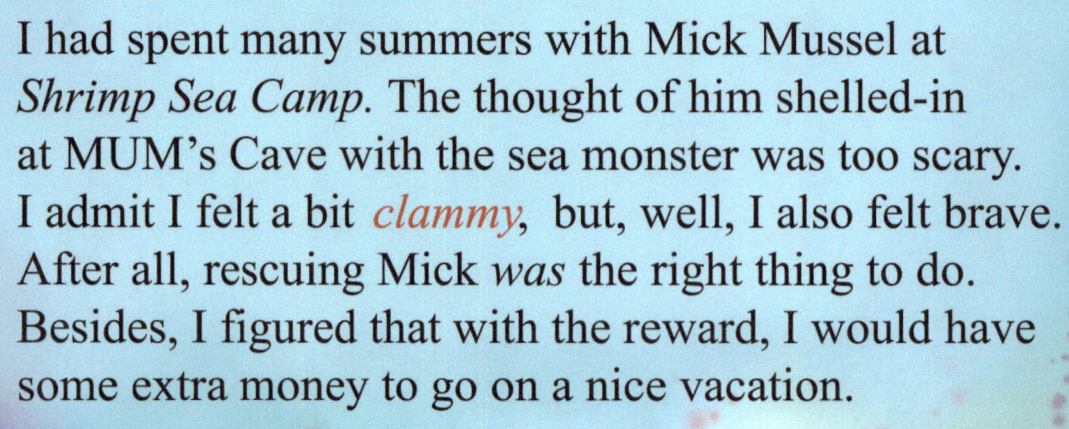

And what's wrong with being a bit clammy?

Once I volunteered, I became the most popular shell ever. Some of my shell friends gathered to give me advice. Some tried to convince me not to go, especially Scallopina, the cockle-shell of my heart. But I set *ashore* my fears, took a deep-water breath, and got ready to set out on my mission.

The Mission

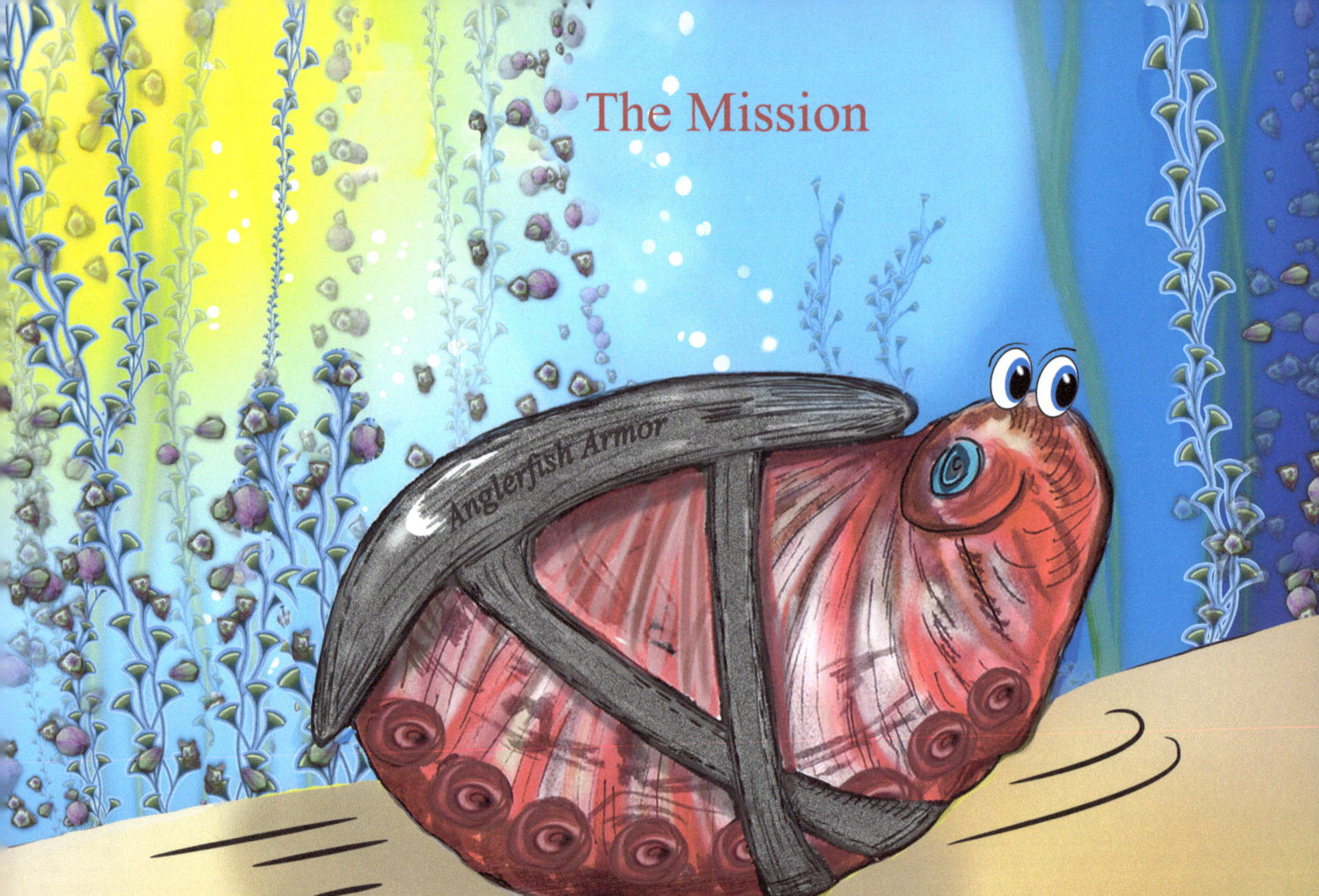

I laughed nervously as they suited me up with armor and sent me on my way. I drifted briskly along the sandy floor as I kept telling myself, *I'm a brave shell . . . I'm a brave shell . . . I'm a brave shell.* As I got farther and farther away from home, I realized that not a single other shell was in sight.

It was so eerily quiet that you could hear a seahorse sigh.

Ho-hum . . . sigh

I bravely floated along as I thought out my rescue plan. Suddenly, I heard a loud SHRIEK. I flipped over and over because of the weight of my armor. I had floated right over a sleeping starfish.

And *floating over a sleeping starfish is never a good idea!*

The starfish jumped up. He stood on his two leg-points and flexed the whale-sized muscles on his arm-points. My armor had loosened from my flipping over, and it shook off my back. I think I almost turned albino-fish white!

Grrrrr! You clumsy shell! Didn't you see me sleeping? I should turn you into shell dust!

I told him, "I'm sorry—it was an accident—I didn't mean to *star*-tle you." The starfish was not amused. I slowly backed away from him, grabbed up my armor, and, without hesitation, floated away as *fassssst* as I could.

I didn't get far before I heard some rustling in the nearby coral. My float became a swim, a shark-like swim at that! I turned around to see if the starfish had followed me, and WHAM! I bumped into a glowing squid with yellow and green tentacles waving like seaweed. Apparently the squid had just returned home after a tiring day at the squidatorium, and he didn't appreciate being disturbed.

And *bumping into a tired squid is never a good idea!*

I didn't get a chance to apologize before he sprayed me with his yucky, **green** squid ink! I flattened out like a sand dollar and took off before he could spray me again.

The Sea Monster

I scraped the squid ink off my armor and out of my eyes.

The water seemed darker and colder. I floated along, and through my still-stinging eyes, I noticed a sign up ahead: "MUM's Cave."

I hoped the sea monster wouldn't be in his cave. I could then just run in, rescue Mick Mussel, and go back home.

I followed the path of soft sand . . .

I continued *past* the cave to check it out. I decided to attack the cave from the back where I saw the sun shining through the water. The bright sun made the cave look much less scary to me. Then, out of the corner of my eye, I saw a huge, golden-brown creature approach. A cold chill ran down my coils. I looked up . . . and up . . . and up. The creature showed his pointy, barracuda-like teeth!

Taken by surprise, I screeched, "Aaaaah!"
The dreaded sea monster was standing
right in front of me!
By the look on his face, the sea monster
looked *equally* surprised to see *me* floating
right in front of him!

And *surprising a sea monster is never a good idea!*

The sea monster's voice ROARED
and *vibrated* through the water.
I looked *up* at him.
He looked *down* at me.
Not knowing what to
expect next, I
froze in place.

Am I hearing correctly? I thought. I listened to the sea monster's loud but friendly words. I relaxed my shell shoulders when I realized I had nothing to fear. The monster meant me no harm!

Finding Mick Mussel

The lonely monster *wanted* and *hoped* to make some small shells his guests. He even decorated one of the rooms of his cave with miniature-sized furniture. I explained to the monster that it was his LOUD and *v-v-vibr-r-rating* roar, his BIG size and scary teeth that scared away all the seashells.

The sea monster led me to a small room at the back of his cave. I followed the monster, but I didn't know what to expect. I found Mick Mussel perched on a fluffy mound of sea moss. While he was chasing a school of minnows, Mick had come upon the sea monster. He had immediately realized the same thing I did. He had nothing to fear. The monster meant him no harm.

Mick said he was having such a great time, he lost track of how long he'd been gone. I couldn't believe it! I had dealt with an angry starfish who wanted to turn me into shell dust, a tired squid who slimed me, and a sea monster who I *thought* was going to give me a major *shell-acking*—and Mick had simply lost track of time!

That's funny Shelty!

Mick was sitting there, relaxing, and drinking a glass of green-fish tea. He'd been reading the classic *The Old Shell and the Sea* to his new friend, Ollie Octopus. A lobster chair and an antique fish-legged table decorated the room. An original starfish plate and a pink-fish pitcher sat on the table top, too!

-23-

I explained to Mick and the sea monster that everyone was worried, especially Mick's father, the Mussel Colony Leader. When the sea monster offered to *carry* us back home, I said "YES, please!" Mick agreed, thinking how much fun being carried home would be. We arrived back home in what seemed like ten giant steps.

My friends didn't think I would return home safe with Mick, having heard such horrible stories about the sea monster. They planned to stay in what we shells call a *hermit-crab huddle* until I returned back home. Scallopina couldn't believe her eyes when she saw Mick and me, safe and sound, being carried home by the sea monster himself. We had fun explaining to our friends that the so-called "sea monster" wasn't a monster at all! He had named his cave **MUM**'s Cave because he felt he was a **MisUnderstood Monster**. We all laughed.

When my friends heard about my run-ins with the starfish who wanted to fight me, the squid who covered me in yucky green squid ink, and then my surprising the unsuspecting giant sea monster, they told me I'd been very brave to have continued the mission.

The Mussel Colony Leader made plans to invite "MUM" to a good old-fashioned seaweed dinner. My shell friends and I promised to visit our new monster friend on a regular basis. And MUM the monster felt magnificent about his many new friends, too!

I became quite popular among my friends, and I know that my great-grandfather would have been pretty proud of me. My adventure even made the front pages of the *Sea Sediment News* and the *Oyster Gazette*! I also received a nifty reward from the Mussel Colony Leader for my bravery. I decided to use the reward money to take this nice vacation here in the Shellhamas.

Whew!
Well, that's my story—the tale
of my first adventure.

Thanks for joining me, everybody! I hope we meet again
when I have my next adventure!

ZZZzzzzz . . .

And so Shelty went back to his well-deserved rest and relaxation
in the Shellhamas. He fell asleep within minutes after Dottie left,
having quite exhausted himself reciting his adventure.

The End